Welcome to our Restroom
Please Get Comfy!

Welcome to our Restroom

Please Seat Yourself!

Name: _____

Visting From: _____

Date: _____ Time: _____

Reason for Visit: _____

During Your Visit Did you...

☐ Play with your smartphone?

☐ Mess with your hair?

☐ Inspect your teeth for food?

☐ Check out your butt in the mirror?

☐ Check your zipper/fly?

☐ Read through this entire guest book?

Your Favorite Name(s) for this Room?

☐ Powder Room   ☐ The office

☐ Crapper   ☐ Can

☐ John   ☐ Other....

Please Tick All That Apply

☐ I take restroom selfies

☐ I snoop in medicine cabinets

☐ I text/call while on the toilet

☐ I pick my nose in the restroom

☐ I talk to myself while on the toilet

Doodles & Brilliant Thoughts Inspired by The Throne

Welcome to our Restroom

Please Seat Yourself!

Name: _____
Visting From: _____
Date: _____ Time: _____
Reason for Visit: _____

During Your Visit Did you...

☐ Play with your smartphone?
☐ Mess with your hair?
☐ Inspect your teeth for food?
☐ Check out your butt in the mirror?
☐ Check your zipper/fly?
☐ Read through this entire guest book?

Your Favorite Name(s) for this Room?

☐ Powder Room   ☐ The office
☐ Crapper   ☐ Can
☐ John   ☐ Other....

Please Tick All That Apply

☐ I take restroom selfies
☐ I snoop in medicine cabinets
☐ I text/call while on the toilet
☐ I pick my nose in the restroom
☐ I talk to myself while on the toilet

Doodles & Brilliant Thoughts Inspired by The Throne

Welcome to our Restroom

Please Seat Yourself!

Name: _____

Visiting From: _____

Date: _____ Time: _____

Reason for Visit: _____

During Your Visit Did you...

☐ Play with your smartphone?

☐ Mess with your hair?

☐ Inspect your teeth for food?

☐ Check out your butt in the mirror?

☐ Check your zipper/fly?

☐ Read through this entire guest book?

Your Favorite Name(s) for this Room?

☐ Powder Room   ☐ The office

☐ Crapper   ☐ Can

☐ John   ☐ Other....

Please Tick All That Apply

☐ I take restroom selfies

☐ I snoop in medicine cabinets

☐ I text/call while on the toilet

☐ I pick my nose in the restroom

☐ I talk to myself while on the toilet

Doodles & Brilliant Thoughts Inspired by The Throne

Welcome to our Restroom
Please Seat Yourself!

Name: _____
Visiting From: _____
Date: _____ Time: _____
Reason for Visit: _____

During Your Visit Did you...

- ☐ Play with your smartphone?
- ☐ Mess with your hair?
- ☐ Inspect your teeth for food?
- ☐ Check out your butt in the mirror?
- ☐ Check your zipper/fly?
- ☐ Read through this entire guest book?

Your Favorite Name(s) for this Room?

- ☐ Powder Room
- ☐ Crapper
- ☐ John
- ☐ The office
- ☐ Can
- ☐ Other....

Please Tick All That Apply

- ☐ I take restroom selfies
- ☐ I snoop in medicine cabinets
- ☐ I text/call while on the toilet
- ☐ I pick my nose in the restroom
- ☐ I talk to myself while on the toilet

Doodles & Brilliant Thoughts Inspired by The Throne

Welcome to our Restroom
Please Seat Yourself!

Name: _____
Visiting From: _____
Date: _____ Time: _____
Reason for Visit: _____

Your Favorite Name(s) for this Room?

☐ Powder Room ☐ The office
☐ Crapper   ☐ Can
☐ John   ☐ Other....

During Your Visit Did you...

☐ Play with your smartphone?
☐ Mess with your hair?
☐ Inspect your teeth for food?
☐ Check out your butt in the mirror?
☐ Check your zipper/fly?
☐ Read through this entire guest book?

Please Tick All That Apply

☐ I take restroom selfies
☐ I snoop in medicine cabinets
☐ I text/call while on the toilet
☐ I pick my nose in the restroom
☐ I talk to myself while on the toilet

Doodles & Brilliant Thoughts Inspired by The Throne

Welcome to our Restroom
Please Seat Yourself!

Name: _____

Visting From: _____

Date: _____ Time: _____

Reason for Visit: _____

During Your Visit Did you...

☐ Play with your smartphone?
☐ Mess with your hair?
☐ Inspect your teeth for food?
☐ Check out your butt in the mirror?
☐ Check your zipper/fly?
☐ Read through this entire guest book?

Your Favorite Name(s) for this Room?

☐ Powder Room   ☐ The office
☐ Crapper   ☐ Can
☐ John   ☐ Other....

Please Tick All That Apply

☐ I take restroom selfies
☐ I snoop in medicine cabinets
☐ I text/call while on the toilet
☐ I pick my nose in the restroom
☐ I talk to myself while on the toilet

Doodles & Brilliant Thoughts Inspired by The Throne

Welcome to our Restroom

Please Seat Yourself!

Name: —————————————
Visiting From: ———————————
Date: ——————— Time: ————————
Reason for Visit: ———————————

During Your Visit Did you...

☐ Play with your smartphone?
☐ Mess with your hair?
☐ Inspect your teeth for food?
☐ Check out your butt in the mirror?
☐ Check your zipper/fly?
☐ Read through this entire guest book?

Your Favorite Name(s) for this Room?

☐ Powder Room   ☐ The office
☐ Crapper   ☐ Can
☐ John   ☐ Other....

Please Tick All That Apply

☐ I take restroom selfies
☐ I snoop in medicine cabinets
☐ I text/call while on the toilet
☐ I pick my nose in the restroom
☐ I talk to myself while on the toilet

Doodles & Brilliant Thoughts Inspired by The Throne

Welcome to our Restroom

Please Seat Yourself!

Name: _____
Visiting From: _____
Date: _____ Time: _____
Reason for Visit: _____

During Your Visit Did you...

☐ Play with your smartphone?
☐ Mess with your hair?
☐ Inspect your teeth for food?
☐ Check out your butt in the mirror?
☐ Check your zipper/fly?
☐ Read through this entire guest book?

Your Favorite Name(s) for this Room?

☐ Powder Room   ☐ The office
☐ Crapper   ☐ Can
☐ John   ☐ Other....

Please Tick All That Apply

☐ I take restroom selfies
☐ I snoop in medicine cabinets
☐ I text/call while on the toilet
☐ I pick my nose in the restroom
☐ I talk to myself while on the toilet

Doodles & Brilliant Thoughts Inspired by The Throne

Welcome to our Restroom

Please Seat Yourself!

Name: _____
Visting From: _____
Date: _____ Time: _____
Reason for Visit: _____

During Your Visit Did you...

☐ Play with your smartphone?
☐ Mess with your hair?
☐ Inspect your teeth for food?
☐ Check out your butt in the mirror?
☐ Check your zipper/fly?
☐ Read through this entire guest book?

Your Favorite Name(s) for this Room?

☐ Powder Room   ☐ The office
☐ Crapper   ☐ Can
☐ John   ☐ Other....

Please Tick All That Apply

☐ I take restroom selfies
☐ I snoop in medicine cabinets
☐ I text/call while on the toilet
☐ I pick my nose in the restroom
☐ I talk to myself while on the toilet

Doodles & Brilliant Thoughts Inspired by The Throne

Welcome to our Restroom
Please Seat Yourself!

Name: ————————————
Visiting From: ————————
Date: —————— Time: ————
Reason for Visit: ——————

During Your Visit Did you...

- ☐ Play with your smartphone?
- ☐ Mess with your hair?
- ☐ Inspect your teeth for food?
- ☐ Check out your butt in the mirror?
- ☐ Check your zipper/fly?
- ☐ Read through this entire guest book?

Your Favorite Name(s) for this Room?

- ☐ Powder Room
- ☐ Crapper
- ☐ John
- ☐ The office
- ☐ Can
- ☐ Other....

Please Tick All That Apply

- ☐ I take restroom selfies
- ☐ I snoop in medicine cabinets
- ☐ I text/call while on the toilet
- ☐ I pick my nose in the restroom
- ☐ I talk to myself while on the toilet

Doodles & Brilliant Thoughts Inspired by The Throne

Welcome to our Restroom

Please Seat Yourself!

Name: ———————————
Visting From: ———————————
Date: ————————— Time: —————————
Reason for Visit: ———————————

During Your Visit Did you...

☐ Play with your smartphone?
☐ Mess with your hair?
☐ Inspect your teeth for food?
☐ Check out your butt in the mirror?
☐ Check your zipper/fly?
☐ Read through this entire guest book?

Your Favorite Name(s) for this Room?

☐ Powder Room   ☐ The office
☐ Crapper   ☐ Can
☐ John   ☐ Other....

Please Tick All That Apply

☐ I take restroom selfies
☐ I snoop in medicine cabinets
☐ I text/call while on the toilet
☐ I pick my nose in the restroom
☐ I talk to myself while on the toilet

Doodles & Brilliant Thoughts Inspired by The Throne

Welcome to our Restroom

Please Seat Yourself!

Name: _____
Visiting From: _____
Date: _____ Time: _____
Reason for Visit: _____

During Your Visit Did you...

- ☐ Play with your smartphone?
- ☐ Mess with your hair?
- ☐ Inspect your teeth for food?
- ☐ Check out your butt in the mirror?
- ☐ Check your zipper/fly?
- ☐ Read through this entire guest book?

Your Favorite Name(s) for this Room?

- ☐ Powder Room
- ☐ Crapper
- ☐ John
- ☐ The office
- ☐ Can
- ☐ Other....

Please Tick All That Apply

- ☐ I take restroom selfies
- ☐ I snoop in medicine cabinets
- ☐ I text/call while on the toilet
- ☐ I pick my nose in the restroom
- ☐ I talk to myself while on the toilet

Doodles & Brilliant Thoughts Inspired by The Throne

Welcome to our Restroom

Please Seat Yourself!

Name: _____
Visting From: _____
Date: _____ Time: _____
Reason for Visit: _____

During Your Visit Did you...

☐ Play with your smartphone?
☐ Mess with your hair?
☐ Inspect your teeth for food?
☐ Check out your butt in the mirror?
☐ Check your zipper/fly?
☐ Read through this entire guest book?

Your Favorite Name(s) for this Room?

☐ Powder Room   ☐ The office
☐ Crapper   ☐ Can
☐ John   ☐ Other....

Please Tick All That Apply

☐ I take restroom selfies
☐ I snoop in medicine cabinets
☐ I text/call while on the toilet
☐ I pick my nose in the restroom
☐ I talk to myself while on the toilet

Doodles & Brilliant Thoughts Inspired by The Throne

Welcome to our Restroom
Please Seat Yourself!

Name: _____
Visting From: _____
Date: _____ Time: _____
Reason for Visit: _____

During Your Visit Did you...
☐ Play with your smartphone?
☐ Mess with your hair?
☐ Inspect your teeth for food?
☐ Check out your butt in the mirror?
☐ Check your zipper/fly?
☐ Read through this entire guest book?

Your Favorite Name(s) for this Room?
☐ Powder Room ☐ The office
☐ Crapper   ☐ Can
☐ John   ☐ Other....

Please Tick All That Apply
☐ I take restroom selfies
☐ I snoop in medicine cabinets
☐ I text/call while on the toilet
☐ I pick my nose in the restroom
☐ I talk to myself while on the toilet

Doodles & Brilliant Thoughts Inspired by The Throne

Welcome to our Restroom

Please Seat Yourself!

Name: _____
Visting From: _____
Date: _____ Time: _____
Reason for Visit: _____

During Your Visit Did you...

- ☐ Play with your smartphone?
- ☐ Mess with your hair?
- ☐ Inspect your teeth for food?
- ☐ Check out your butt in the mirror?
- ☐ Check your zipper/fly?
- ☐ Read through this entire guest book?

Your Favorite Name(s) for this Room?

- ☐ Powder Room
- ☐ Crapper
- ☐ John
- ☐ The office
- ☐ Can
- ☐ Other....

Please Tick All That Apply

- ☐ I take restroom selfies
- ☐ I snoop in medicine cabinets
- ☐ I text/call while on the toilet
- ☐ I pick my nose in the restroom
- ☐ I talk to myself while on the toilet

Doodles & Brilliant Thoughts Inspired by The Throne

Welcome to our Restroom
Please Seat Yourself!

Name: _____

Visiting From: _____

Date: _____ Time: _____

Reason for Visit: _____

During Your Visit Did you...

☐ Play with your smartphone?

☐ Mess with your hair?

☐ Inspect your teeth for food?

☐ Check out your butt in the mirror?

☐ Check your zipper/fly?

☐ Read through this entire guest book?

Your Favorite Name(s) for this Room?

☐ Powder Room   ☐ The office

☐ Crapper   ☐ Can

☐ John   ☐ Other....

Please Tick All That Apply

☐ I take restroom selfies

☐ I snoop in medicine cabinets

☐ I text/call while on the toilet

☐ I pick my nose in the restroom

☐ I talk to myself while on the toilet

Doodles & Brilliant Thoughts Inspired by The Throne

Welcome to our Restroom
Please Seat Yourself!

Name: —————————————————
Visting From: —————————————
Date: ———————— Time: ————————
Reason for Visit: —————————————

During Your Visit Did you...

☐ Play with your smartphone?
☐ Mess with your hair?
☐ Inspect your teeth for food?
☐ Check out your butt in the mirror?
☐ Check your zipper/fly?
☐ Read through this entire guest book?

Your Favorite Name(s) for this Room?

☐ Powder Room   ☐ The office
☐ Crapper   ☐ Can
☐ John   ☐ Other....

Please Tick All That Apply

☐ I take restroom selfies
☐ I snoop in medicine cabinets
☐ I text/call while on the toilet
☐ I pick my nose in the restroom
☐ I talk to myself while on the toilet

Doodles & Brilliant Thoughts Inspired by The Throne

Welcome to our Restroom

Please Seat Yourself!

Name: _____
Visting From: _____
Date: _____ Time: _____
Reason for Visit: _____

During Your Visit Did you...

☐ Play with your smartphone?
☐ Mess with your hair?
☐ Inspect your teeth for food?
☐ Check out your butt in the mirror?
☐ Check your zipper/fly?
☐ Read through this entire guest book?

Your Favorite Name(s) for this Room?

☐ Powder Room ☐ The office
☐ Crapper   ☐ Can
☐ John   ☐ Other....

Please Tick All That Apply

☐ I take restroom selfies
☐ I snoop in medicine cabinets
☐ I text/call while on the toilet
☐ I pick my nose in the restroom
☐ I talk to myself while on the toilet

Doodles & Brilliant Thoughts Inspired by The Throne

Welcome to our Restroom

Please Seat Yourself!

Name: _____
Visting From: _____
Date: _____ Time: _____
Reason for Visit: _____

During Your Visit Did you...

☐ Play with your smartphone?
☐ Mess with your hair?
☐ Inspect your teeth for food?
☐ Check out your butt in the mirror?
☐ Check your zipper/fly?
☐ Read through this entire guest book?

Your Favorite Name(s) for this Room?

☐ Powder Room   ☐ The office
☐ Crapper   ☐ Can
☐ John   ☐ Other....

Please Tick All That Apply

☐ I take restroom selfies
☐ I snoop in medicine cabinets
☐ I text/call while on the toilet
☐ I pick my nose in the restroom
☐ I talk to myself while on the toilet

Doodles & Brilliant Thoughts Inspired by The Throne

Welcome to our Restroom
Please Seat Yourself!

Name: _____
Visting From: _____
Date: _____ Time: _____
Reason for Visit: _____

During Your Visit Did you...

☐ Play with your smartphone?
☐ Mess with your hair?
☐ Inspect your teeth for food?
☐ Check out your butt in the mirror?
☐ Check your zipper/fly?
☐ Read through this entire guest book?

Your Favorite Name(s) for this Room?

☐ Powder Room   ☐ The office
☐ Crapper   ☐ Can
☐ John   ☐ Other....

Please Tick All That Apply

☐ I take restroom selfies
☐ I snoop in medicine cabinets
☐ I text/call while on the toilet
☐ I pick my nose in the restroom
☐ I talk to myself while on the toilet

Doodles & Brilliant Thoughts Inspired by The Throne

Welcome to our Restroom

Please Seat Yourself!

Name: ―――――――――――――
Visiting From: ―――――――――――
Date: ――――――― Time: ―――――――
Reason for Visit: ―――――――――――

During Your Visit Did you...

☐ Play with your smartphone?
☐ Mess with your hair?
☐ Inspect your teeth for food?
☐ Check out your butt in the mirror?
☐ Check your zipper/fly?
☐ Read through this entire guest book?

Your Favorite Name(s) for this Room?

☐ Powder Room   ☐ The office
☐ Crapper   ☐ Can
☐ John   ☐ Other....

Please Tick All That Apply

☐ I take restroom selfies
☐ I snoop in medicine cabinets
☐ I text/call while on the toilet
☐ I pick my nose in the restroom
☐ I talk to myself while on the toilet

Doodles & Brilliant Thoughts Inspired by The Throne

Welcome to our Restroom
Please Seat Yourself!

Name: _____
Visting From: _____
Date: _____ Time: _____
Reason for Visit: _____

During Your Visit Did you...

- ☐ Play with your smartphone?
- ☐ Mess with your hair?
- ☐ Inspect your teeth for food?
- ☐ Check out your butt in the mirror?
- ☐ Check your zipper/fly?
- ☐ Read through this entire guest book?

Your Favorite Name(s) for this Room?

- ☐ Powder Room
- ☐ Crapper
- ☐ John
- ☐ The office
- ☐ Can
- ☐ Other....

Please Tick All That Apply

- ☐ I take restroom selfies
- ☐ I snoop in medicine cabinets
- ☐ I text/call while on the toilet
- ☐ I pick my nose in the restroom
- ☐ I talk to myself while on the toilet

Doodles & Brilliant Thoughts Inspired by The Throne

Welcome to our Restroom
Please Seat Yourself!

Name: _____
Visting From: _____
Date: _____ Time: _____
Reason for Visit: _____

During Your Visit Did you...

☐ Play with your smartphone?
☐ Mess with your hair?
☐ Inspect your teeth for food?
☐ Check out your butt in the mirror?
☐ Check your zipper/fly?
☐ Read through this entire guest book?

Your Favorite Name(s) for this Room?

☐ Powder Room   ☐ The office
☐ Crapper   ☐ Can
☐ John   ☐ Other....

Please Tick All That Apply

☐ I take restroom selfies
☐ I snoop in medicine cabinets
☐ I text/call while on the toilet
☐ I pick my nose in the restroom
☐ I talk to myself while on the toilet

Doodles & Brilliant Thoughts Inspired by The Throne

Welcome to our Restroom
Please Seat Yourself!

Name: ───────────────
Visting From: ───────────
Date: ──────── Time: ────────
Reason for Visit: ───────────

During Your Visit Did you...

- ☐ Play with your smartphone?
- ☐ Mess with your hair?
- ☐ Inspect your teeth for food?
- ☐ Check out your butt in the mirror?
- ☐ Check your zipper/fly?
- ☐ Read through this entire guest book?

Your Favorite Name(s) for this Room?

- ☐ Powder Room
- ☐ Crapper
- ☐ John
- ☐ The office
- ☐ Can
- ☐ Other....

Please Tick All That Apply

- ☐ I take restroom selfies
- ☐ I snoop in medicine cabinets
- ☐ I text/call while on the toilet
- ☐ I pick my nose in the restroom
- ☐ I talk to myself while on the toilet

Doodles & Brilliant Thoughts Inspired by The Throne

Welcome to our Restroom

Please Seat Yourself!

Name: _____
Visiting From: _____
Date: _____ Time: _____
Reason for Visit: _____

During Your Visit Did you...

☐ Play with your smartphone?
☐ Mess with your hair?
☐ Inspect your teeth for food?
☐ Check out your butt in the mirror?
☐ Check your zipper/fly?
☐ Read through this entire guest book?

Your Favorite Name(s) for this Room?

☐ Powder Room
☐ Crapper
☐ John
☐ The office
☐ Can
☐ Other....

Please Tick All That Apply

☐ I take restroom selfies
☐ I snoop in medicine cabinets
☐ I text/call while on the toilet
☐ I pick my nose in the restroom
☐ I talk to myself while on the toilet

Doodles & Brilliant Thoughts Inspired by The Throne

Welcome to our Restroom

Please Seat Yourself!

Name: _____
Visting From: _____
Date: _____ Time: _____
Reason for Visit: _____

During Your Visit Did you...

☐ Play with your smartphone?
☐ Mess with your hair?
☐ Inspect your teeth for food?
☐ Check out your butt in the mirror?
☐ Check your zipper/fly?
☐ Read through this entire guest book?

Your Favorite Name(s) for this Room?

☐ Powder Room   ☐ The office
☐ Crapper   ☐ Can
☐ John   ☐ Other....

Please Tick All That Apply

☐ I take restroom selfies
☐ I snoop in medicine cabinets
☐ I text/call while on the toilet
☐ I pick my nose in the restroom
☐ I talk to myself while on the toilet

Doodles & Brilliant Thoughts Inspired by The Throne

Welcome to our Restroom

Please Seat Yourself!

Name: —————————————————
Visiting From: ———————————————
Date: ——————————— Time: ——————————
Reason for Visit: ——————————————

During Your Visit Did you...

☐ Play with your smartphone?
☐ Mess with your hair?
☐ Inspect your teeth for food?
☐ Check out your butt in the mirror?
☐ Check your zipper/fly?
☐ Read through this entire guest book?

Your Favorite Name(s) for this Room?

☐ Powder Room
☐ Crapper
☐ John
☐ The office
☐ Can
☐ Other....

Please Tick All That Apply

☐ I take restroom selfies
☐ I snoop in medicine cabinets
☐ I text/call while on the toilet
☐ I pick my nose in the restroom
☐ I talk to myself while on the toilet

Doodles & Brilliant Thoughts Inspired by The Throne

Welcome to our Restroom

Please Seat Yourself!

Name: _____

Visting From: _____

Date: _____ Time: _____

Reason for Visit: _____

During Your Visit Did you...

☐ Play with your smartphone?

☐ Mess with your hair?

☐ Inspect your teeth for food?

☐ Check out your butt in the mirror?

☐ Check your zipper/fly?

☐ Read through this entire guest book?

Your Favorite Name(s) for this Room?

☐ Powder Room   ☐ The office

☐ Crapper   ☐ Can

☐ John   ☐ Other....

Please Tick All That Apply

☐ I take restroom selfies

☐ I snoop in medicine cabinets

☐ I text/call while on the toilet

☐ I pick my nose in the restroom

☐ I talk to myself while on the toilet

Doodles & Brilliant Thoughts Inspired by The Throne

Welcome to our Restroom

Please Seat Yourself!

Name: _____
Visiting From: _____
Date: _____ Time: _____
Reason for Visit: _____

During Your Visit Did you...

☐ Play with your smartphone?
☐ Mess with your hair?
☐ Inspect your teeth for food?
☐ Check out your butt in the mirror?
☐ Check your zipper/fly?
☐ Read through this entire guest book?

Your Favorite Name(s) for this Room?

☐ Powder Room
☐ Crapper
☐ John
☐ The office
☐ Can
☐ Other....

Please Tick All That Apply

☐ I take restroom selfies
☐ I snoop in medicine cabinets
☐ I text/call while on the toilet
☐ I pick my nose in the restroom
☐ I talk to myself while on the toilet

Doodles & Brilliant Thoughts Inspired by The Throne

Welcome to our Restroom
Please Seat Yourself!

Name: _____
Visiting From: _____
Date: _____ Time: _____
Reason for Visit: _____

During Your Visit Did you...

☐ Play with your smartphone?
☐ Mess with your hair?
☐ Inspect your teeth for food?
☐ Check out your butt in the mirror?
☐ Check your zipper/fly?
☐ Read through this entire guest book?

Your Favorite Name(s) for this Room?

☐ Powder Room   ☐ The office
☐ Crapper   ☐ Can
☐ John   ☐ Other....

Please Tick All That Apply

☐ I take restroom selfies
☐ I snoop in medicine cabinets
☐ I text/call while on the toilet
☐ I pick my nose in the restroom
☐ I talk to myself while on the toilet

Doodles & Brilliant Thoughts Inspired by The Throne

Welcome to our Restroom

Please Seat Yourself!

Name: _____

Visiting From: _____

Date: _____ Time: _____

Reason for Visit: _____

During Your Visit Did you...

- ☐ Play with your smartphone?
- ☐ Mess with your hair?
- ☐ Inspect your teeth for food?
- ☐ Check out your butt in the mirror?
- ☐ Check your zipper/fly?
- ☐ Read through this entire guest book?

Your Favorite Name(s) for this Room?

- ☐ Powder Room
- ☐ Crapper
- ☐ John
- ☐ The office
- ☐ Can
- ☐ Other....

Please Tick All That Apply

- ☐ I take restroom selfies
- ☐ I snoop in medicine cabinets
- ☐ I text/call while on the toilet
- ☐ I pick my nose in the restroom
- ☐ I talk to myself while on the toilet

Doodles & Brilliant Thoughts Inspired by The Throne

Welcome to our Restroom
Please Seat Yourself!

Name: _____
Visting From: _____
Date: _____ Time: _____
Reason for Visit: _____

During Your Visit Did you...

- ☐ Play with your smartphone?
- ☐ Mess with your hair?
- ☐ Inspect your teeth for food?
- ☐ Check out your butt in the mirror?
- ☐ Check your zipper/fly?
- ☐ Read through this entire guest book?

Your Favorite Name(s) for this Room?

- ☐ Powder Room
- ☐ Crapper
- ☐ John
- ☐ The office
- ☐ Can
- ☐ Other....

Please Tick All That Apply

- ☐ I take restroom selfies
- ☐ I snoop in medicine cabinets
- ☐ I text/call while on the toilet
- ☐ I pick my nose in the restroom
- ☐ I talk to myself while on the toilet

Doodles & Brilliant Thoughts Inspired by The Throne

Welcome to our Restroom
Please Seat Yourself!

Name: ─────────────────
Visting From: ─────────────
Date: ───────── Time: ─────────
Reason for Visit: ──────────────

During Your Visit Did you...

☐ Play with your smartphone?
☐ Mess with your hair?
☐ Inspect your teeth for food?
☐ Check out your butt in the mirror?
☐ Check your zipper/fly?
☐ Read through this entire guest book?

Your Favorite Name(s) for this Room?

☐ Powder Room   ☐ The office
☐ Crapper   ☐ Can
☐ John   ☐ Other....

Please Tick All That Apply

☐ I take restroom selfies
☐ I snoop in medicine cabinets
☐ I text/call while on the toilet
☐ I pick my nose in the restroom
☐ I talk to myself while on the toilet

Doodles & Brilliant Thoughts Inspired by The Throne

Welcome to our Restroom
Please Seat Yourself!

Name: _____
Visting From: _____
Date: _____ Time: _____
Reason for Visit: _____

During Your Visit Did you...

- [ ] Play with your smartphone?
- [ ] Mess with your hair?
- [ ] Inspect your teeth for food?
- [ ] Check out your butt in the mirror?
- [ ] Check your zipper/fly?
- [ ] Read through this entire guest book?

Your Favorite Name(s) for this Room?

- [ ] Powder Room
- [ ] Crapper
- [ ] John
- [ ] The office
- [ ] Can
- [ ] Other....

Please Tick All That Apply

- [ ] I take restroom selfies
- [ ] I snoop in medicine cabinets
- [ ] I text/call while on the toilet
- [ ] I pick my nose in the restroom
- [ ] I talk to myself while on the toilet

Doodles & Brilliant Thoughts Inspired by The Throne

Welcome to our Restroom
Please Seat Yourself!

Name: —————————————
Visting From: —————————————
Date: ————————— Time: —————————
Reason for Visit: —————————————

During Your Visit Did you...

- [ ] Play with your smartphone?
- [ ] Mess with your hair?
- [ ] Inspect your teeth for food?
- [ ] Check out your butt in the mirror?
- [ ] Check your zipper/fly?
- [ ] Read through this entire guest book?

Your Favorite Name(s) for this Room?

- [ ] Powder Room
- [ ] Crapper
- [ ] John
- [ ] The office
- [ ] Can
- [ ] Other....

Please Tick All That Apply

- [ ] I take restroom selfies
- [ ] I snoop in medicine cabinets
- [ ] I text/call while on the toilet
- [ ] I pick my nose in the restroom
- [ ] I talk to myself while on the toilet

Doodles & Brilliant Thoughts Inspired by The Throne

Welcome to our Restroom
Please Seat Yourself!

Name: _____
Visting From: _____
Date: _____ Time: _____
Reason for Visit: _____

During Your Visit Did you...

- ☐ Play with your smartphone?
- ☐ Mess with your hair?
- ☐ Inspect your teeth for food?
- ☐ Check out your butt in the mirror?
- ☐ Check your zipper/fly?
- ☐ Read through this entire guest book?

Your Favorite Name(s) for this Room?

- ☐ Powder Room
- ☐ Crapper
- ☐ John
- ☐ The office
- ☐ Can
- ☐ Other....

Please Tick All That Apply

- ☐ I take restroom selfies
- ☐ I snoop in medicine cabinets
- ☐ I text/call while on the toilet
- ☐ I pick my nose in the restroom
- ☐ I talk to myself while on the toilet

Doodles & Brilliant Thoughts Inspired by The Throne

Welcome to our Restroom
Please Seat Yourself!

Name: —————————————————
Visting From: —————————————
Date: ——————— Time: —————————
Reason for Visit: ——————————

During Your Visit Did you...

- ☐ Play with your smartphone?
- ☐ Mess with your hair?
- ☐ Inspect your teeth for food?
- ☐ Check out your butt in the mirror?
- ☐ Check your zipper/fly?
- ☐ Read through this entire guest book?

Your Favorite Name(s) for this Room?

- ☐ Powder Room
- ☐ Crapper
- ☐ John
- ☐ The office
- ☐ Can
- ☐ Other....

Please Tick All That Apply

- ☐ I take restroom selfies
- ☐ I snoop in medicine cabinets
- ☐ I text/call while on the toilet
- ☐ I pick my nose in the restroom
- ☐ I talk to myself while on the toilet

Doodles & Brilliant Thoughts Inspired by The Throne

Welcome to our Restroom
Please Seat Yourself!

Name: _____
Visting From: _____
Date: _____ Time: _____
Reason for Visit: _____

Your Favorite Name(s) for this Room?

- ☐ Powder Room
- ☐ Crapper
- ☐ John
- ☐ The office
- ☐ Can
- ☐ Other....

During Your Visit Did you...

- ☐ Play with your smartphone?
- ☐ Mess with your hair?
- ☐ Inspect your teeth for food?
- ☐ Check out your butt in the mirror?
- ☐ Check your zipper/fly?
- ☐ Read through this entire guest book?

Please Tick All That Apply

- ☐ I take restroom selfies
- ☐ I snoop in medicine cabinets
- ☐ I text/call while on the toilet
- ☐ I pick my nose in the restroom
- ☐ I talk to myself while on the toilet

Doodles & Brilliant Thoughts Inspired by The Throne

Welcome to our Restroom
Please Seat Yourself!

Name: _____
Visiting From: _____
Date: _____ Time: _____
Reason for Visit: _____

During Your Visit Did you...

☐ Play with your smartphone?
☐ Mess with your hair?
☐ Inspect your teeth for food?
☐ Check out your butt in the mirror?
☐ Check your zipper/fly?
☐ Read through this entire guest book?

Your Favorite Name(s) for this Room?

☐ Powder Room   ☐ The office
☐ Crapper   ☐ Can
☐ John   ☐ Other....

Please Tick All That Apply

☐ I take restroom selfies
☐ I snoop in medicine cabinets
☐ I text/call while on the toilet
☐ I pick my nose in the restroom
☐ I talk to myself while on the toilet

Doodles & Brilliant Thoughts Inspired by The Throne

Welcome to our Restroom

Please Seat Yourself!

Name: —————————————
Visting From: —————————————
Date: ——————— Time: ———————
Reason for Visit: —————————————

During Your Visit Did you...

☐ Play with your smartphone?
☐ Mess with your hair?
☐ Inspect your teeth for food?
☐ Check out your butt in the mirror?
☐ Check your zipper/fly?
☐ Read through this entire guest book?

Your Favorite Name(s) for this Room?

☐ Powder Room   ☐ The office
☐ Crapper   ☐ Can
☐ John   ☐ Other....

Please Tick All That Apply

☐ I take restroom selfies
☐ I snoop in medicine cabinets
☐ I text/call while on the toilet
☐ I pick my nose in the restroom
☐ I talk to myself while on the toilet

Doodles & Brilliant Thoughts Inspired by The Throne

Welcome to our Restroom

Please Seat Yourself!

Name: _____

Visting From: _____

Date: _____ Time: _____

Reason for Visit: _____

During Your Visit Did you...

☐ Play with your smartphone?

☐ Mess with your hair?

☐ Inspect your teeth for food?

☐ Check out your butt in the mirror?

☐ Check your zipper/fly?

☐ Read through this entire guest book?

Your Favorite Name(s) for this Room?

☐ Powder Room   ☐ The office

☐ Crapper   ☐ Can

☐ John   ☐ Other....

Please Tick All That Apply

☐ I take restroom selfies

☐ I snoop in medicine cabinets

☐ I text/call while on the toilet

☐ I pick my nose in the restroom

☐ I talk to myself while on the toilet

Doodles & Brilliant Thoughts Inspired by The Throne

Welcome to our Restroom
Please Seat Yourself!

Name: _____
Visting From: _____
Date: _____ Time: _____
Reason for Visit: _____

During Your Visit Did you...

- [ ] Play with your smartphone?
- [ ] Mess with your hair?
- [ ] Inspect your teeth for food?
- [ ] Check out your butt in the mirror?
- [ ] Check your zipper/fly?
- [ ] Read through this entire guest book?

Your Favorite Name(s) for this Room?

- [ ] Powder Room
- [ ] Crapper
- [ ] John
- [ ] The office
- [ ] Can
- [ ] Other....

Please Tick All That Apply

- [ ] I take restroom selfies
- [ ] I snoop in medicine cabinets
- [ ] I text/call while on the toilet
- [ ] I pick my nose in the restroom
- [ ] I talk to myself while on the toilet

Doodles & Brilliant Thoughts Inspired by The Throne

Welcome to our Restroom

Please Seat Yourself!

Name: ————————————————
Visting From: ————————————————
Date: ———————— Time: ————————
Reason for Visit: ————————————

During Your Visit Did you...

☐ Play with your smartphone?
☐ Mess with your hair?
☐ Inspect your teeth for food?
☐ Check out your butt in the mirror?
☐ Check your zipper/fly?
☐ Read through this entire guest book?

Your Favorite Name(s) for this Room?

☐ Powder Room   ☐ The office
☐ Crapper   ☐ Can
☐ John   ☐ Other....

Please Tick All That Apply

☐ I take restroom selfies
☐ I snoop in medicine cabinets
☐ I text/call while on the toilet
☐ I pick my nose in the restroom
☐ I talk to myself while on the toilet

Doodles & Brilliant Thoughts Inspired by The Throne

Welcome to our Restroom
Please Seat Yourself!

Name: _____
Visting From: _____
Date: _____ Time: _____
Reason for Visit: _____

During Your Visit Did you...

☐ Play with your smartphone?
☐ Mess with your hair?
☐ Inspect your teeth for food?
☐ Check out your butt in the mirror?
☐ Check your zipper/fly?
☐ Read through this entire guest book?

Your Favorite Name(s) for this Room?

☐ Powder Room   ☐ The office
☐ Crapper   ☐ Can
☐ John   ☐ Other....

Please Tick All That Apply

☐ I take restroom selfies
☐ I snoop in medicine cabinets
☐ I text/call while on the toilet
☐ I pick my nose in the restroom
☐ I talk to myself while on the toilet

Doodles & Brilliant Thoughts Inspired by The Throne

Welcome to our Restroom

Please Seat Yourself!

Name: _____
Visting From: _____
Date: _____ Time: _____
Reason for Visit: _____

During Your Visit Did you...

☐ Play with your smartphone?
☐ Mess with your hair?
☐ Inspect your teeth for food?
☐ Check out your butt in the mirror?
☐ Check your zipper/fly?
☐ Read through this entire guest book?

Your Favorite Name(s) for this Room?

☐ Powder Room
☐ Crapper
☐ John
☐ The office
☐ Can
☐ Other....

Please Tick All That Apply

☐ I take restroom selfies
☐ I snoop in medicine cabinets
☐ I text/call while on the toilet
☐ I pick my nose in the restroom
☐ I talk to myself while on the toilet

Doodles & Brilliant Thoughts Inspired by The Throne

Welcome to our Restroom
Please Seat Yourself!

Name: _____
Visting From: _____
Date: _____ Time: _____
Reason for Visit: _____

During Your Visit Did you...

☐ Play with your smartphone?
☐ Mess with your hair?
☐ Inspect your teeth for food?
☐ Check out your butt in the mirror?
☐ Check your zipper/fly?
☐ Read through this entire guest book?

Your Favorite Name(s) for this Room?

☐ Powder Room   ☐ The office
☐ Crapper   ☐ Can
☐ John   ☐ Other....

Please Tick All That Apply

☐ I take restroom selfies
☐ I snoop in medicine cabinets
☐ I text/call while on the toilet
☐ I pick my nose in the restroom
☐ I talk to myself while on the toilet

Doodles & Brilliant Thoughts Inspired by The Throne

Welcome to our Restroom

Please Seat Yourself!

Name: _____
Visting From: _____
Date: _____ Time: _____
Reason for Visit: _____

During Your Visit Did you...

☐ Play with your smartphone?
☐ Mess with your hair?
☐ Inspect your teeth for food?
☐ Check out your butt in the mirror?
☐ Check your zipper/fly?
☐ Read through this entire guest book?

Your Favorite Name(s) for this Room?

☐ Powder Room
☐ Crapper
☐ John
☐ The office
☐ Can
☐ Other....

Please Tick All That Apply

☐ I take restroom selfies
☐ I snoop in medicine cabinets
☐ I text/call while on the toilet
☐ I pick my nose in the restroom
☐ I talk to myself while on the toilet

Doodles & Brilliant Thoughts Inspired by The Throne

Welcome to our Restroom
Please Seat Yourself!

Name: _____

Visting From: _____

Date: _____ Time: _____

Reason for Visit: _____

During Your Visit Did you...

☐ Play with your smartphone?
☐ Mess with your hair?
☐ Inspect your teeth for food?
☐ Check out your butt in the mirror?
☐ Check your zipper/fly?
☐ Read through this entire guest book?

Your Favorite Name(s) for this Room?

☐ Powder Room   ☐ The office
☐ Crapper   ☐ Can
☐ John   ☐ Other....

Please Tick All That Apply

☐ I take restroom selfies
☐ I snoop in medicine cabinets
☐ I text/call while on the toilet
☐ I pick my nose in the restroom
☐ I talk to myself while on the toilet

Doodles & Brilliant Thoughts Inspired by The Throne

Welcome to our Restroom
Please Seat Yourself!

Name: _____
Visting From: _____
Date: _____ Time: _____
Reason for Visit: _____

During Your Visit Did you...

☐ Play with your smartphone?
☐ Mess with your hair?
☐ Inspect your teeth for food?
☐ Check out your butt in the mirror?
☐ Check your zipper/fly?
☐ Read through this entire guest book?

Your Favorite Name(s) for this Room?

☐ Powder Room   ☐ The office
☐ Crapper   ☐ Can
☐ John   ☐ Other....

Please Tick All That Apply

☐ I take restroom selfies
☐ I snoop in medicine cabinets
☐ I text/call while on the toilet
☐ I pick my nose in the restroom
☐ I talk to myself while on the toilet

Doodles & Brilliant Thoughts Inspired by The Throne

Welcome to our Restroom
Please Seat Yourself!

Name: _____

Visting From: _____

Date: _____ Time: _____

Reason for Visit: _____

During Your Visit Did you...

- ☐ Play with your smartphone?
- ☐ Mess with your hair?
- ☐ Inspect your teeth for food?
- ☐ Check out your butt in the mirror?
- ☐ Check your zipper/fly?
- ☐ Read through this entire guest book?

Your Favorite Name(s) for this Room?

- ☐ Powder Room
- ☐ Crapper
- ☐ John
- ☐ The office
- ☐ Can
- ☐ Other....

Please Tick All That Apply

- ☐ I take restroom selfies
- ☐ I snoop in medicine cabinets
- ☐ I text/call while on the toilet
- ☐ I pick my nose in the restroom
- ☐ I talk to myself while on the toilet

Doodles & Brilliant Thoughts Inspired by The Throne

Welcome to our Restroom

Please Seat Yourself!

Name: _____

Visiting From: _____

Date: _____ Time: _____

Reason for Visit: _____

During Your Visit Did you...

- ☐ Play with your smartphone?
- ☐ Mess with your hair?
- ☐ Inspect your teeth for food?
- ☐ Check out your butt in the mirror?
- ☐ Check your zipper/fly?
- ☐ Read through this entire guest book?

Your Favorite Name(s) for this Room?

- ☐ Powder Room
- ☐ Crapper
- ☐ John
- ☐ The office
- ☐ Can
- ☐ Other....

Please Tick All That Apply

- ☐ I take restroom selfies
- ☐ I snoop in medicine cabinets
- ☐ I text/call while on the toilet
- ☐ I pick my nose in the restroom
- ☐ I talk to myself while on the toilet

Doodles & Brilliant Thoughts Inspired by The Throne

Welcome to our Restroom
Please Seat Yourself!

Name: _____
Visting From: _____
Date: _____ Time: _____
Reason for Visit: _____

During Your Visit Did you...

☐ Play with your smartphone?
☐ Mess with your hair?
☐ Inspect your teeth for food?
☐ Check out your butt in the mirror?
☐ Check your zipper/fly?
☐ Read through this entire guest book?

Your Favorite Name(s) for this Room?

☐ Powder Room   ☐ The office
☐ Crapper   ☐ Can
☐ John   ☐ Other....

Please Tick All That Apply

☐ I take restroom selfies
☐ I snoop in medicine cabinets
☐ I text/call while on the toilet
☐ I pick my nose in the restroom
☐ I talk to myself while on the toilet

Doodles & Brilliant Thoughts Inspired by The Throne

Welcome to our Restroom
Please Seat Yourself!

Name: ―――――――――――――
Visting From: ―――――――――――
Date: ―――――――― Time: ―――――――
Reason for Visit: ―――――――――――

During Your Visit Did you...

☐ Play with your smartphone?
☐ Mess with your hair?
☐ Inspect your teeth for food?
☐ Check out your butt in the mirror?
☐ Check your zipper/fly?
☐ Read through this entire guest book?

Your Favorite Name(s) for this Room?

☐ Powder Room   ☐ The office
☐ Crapper   ☐ Can
☐ John   ☐ Other....

Please Tick All That Apply

☐ I take restroom selfies
☐ I snoop in medicine cabinets
☐ I text/call while on the toilet
☐ I pick my nose in the restroom
☐ I talk to myself while on the toilet

Doodles & Brilliant Thoughts Inspired by The Throne

Welcome to our Restroom
Please Seat Yourself!

Name: ————————————————
Visting From: ——————————————
Date: ———————— Time: ——————
Reason for Visit: ——————————————

During Your Visit Did you...

☐ Play with your smartphone?
☐ Mess with your hair?
☐ Inspect your teeth for food?
☐ Check out your butt in the mirror?
☐ Check your zipper/fly?
☐ Read through this entire guest book?

Your Favorite Name(s) for this Room?

☐ Powder Room   ☐ The office
☐ Crapper   ☐ Can
☐ John   ☐ Other....

Please Tick All That Apply

☐ I take restroom selfies
☐ I snoop in medicine cabinets
☐ I text/call while on the toilet
☐ I pick my nose in the restroom
☐ I talk to myself while on the toilet

Doodles & Brilliant Thoughts Inspired by The Throne

Welcome to our Restroom
Please Seat Yourself!

Name: _____
Visiting From: _____
Date: _____ Time: _____
Reason for Visit: _____

During Your Visit Did you...

- [ ] Play with your smartphone?
- [ ] Mess with your hair?
- [ ] Inspect your teeth for food?
- [ ] Check out your butt in the mirror?
- [ ] Check your zipper/fly?
- [ ] Read through this entire guest book?

Your Favorite Name(s) for this Room?

- [ ] Powder Room
- [ ] Crapper
- [ ] John
- [ ] The office
- [ ] Can
- [ ] Other....

Please Tick All That Apply

- [ ] I take restroom selfies
- [ ] I snoop in medicine cabinets
- [ ] I text/call while on the toilet
- [ ] I pick my nose in the restroom
- [ ] I talk to myself while on the toilet

Doodles & Brilliant Thoughts Inspired by The Throne

Welcome to our Restroom
Please Seat Yourself!

Name: _____
Visting From: _____
Date: _____ Time: _____
Reason for Visit: _____

During Your Visit Did you...

- ☐ Play with your smartphone?
- ☐ Mess with your hair?
- ☐ Inspect your teeth for food?
- ☐ Check out your butt in the mirror?
- ☐ Check your zipper/fly?
- ☐ Read through this entire guest book?

Your Favorite Name(s) for this Room?

- ☐ Powder Room
- ☐ Crapper
- ☐ John
- ☐ The office
- ☐ Can
- ☐ Other....

Please Tick All That Apply

- ☐ I take restroom selfies
- ☐ I snoop in medicine cabinets
- ☐ I text/call while on the toilet
- ☐ I pick my nose in the restroom
- ☐ I talk to myself while on the toilet

Doodles & Brilliant Thoughts Inspired by The Throne

Welcome to our Restroom

Please Seat Yourself!

Name: ————————————————

Visting From: ————————————

Date: ———————— Time: ————————

Reason for Visit: ——————————————

During Your Visit Did you...

☐ Play with your smartphone?
☐ Mess with your hair?
☐ Inspect your teeth for food?
☐ Check out your butt in the mirror?
☐ Check your zipper/fly?
☐ Read through this entire guest book?

Your Favorite Name(s) for this Room?

☐ Powder Room
☐ Crapper
☐ John

☐ The office
☐ Can
☐ Other....

Please Tick All That Apply

☐ I take restroom selfies
☐ I snoop in medicine cabinets
☐ I text/call while on the toilet
☐ I pick my nose in the restroom
☐ I talk to myself while on the toilet

Doodles & Brilliant Thoughts Inspired by The Throne

Welcome to our Restroom
Please Seat Yourself!

Name: ————————————————
Visting From: ————————————
Date: ———————— Time: ————————
Reason for Visit: ————————————

During Your Visit Did you...

☐ Play with your smartphone?
☐ Mess with your hair?
☐ Inspect your teeth for food?
☐ Check out your butt in the mirror?
☐ Check your zipper/fly?
☐ Read through this entire guest book?

Your Favorite Name(s) for this Room?

☐ Powder Room   ☐ The office
☐ Crapper   ☐ Can
☐ John   ☐ Other....

Please Tick All That Apply

☐ I take restroom selfies
☐ I snoop in medicine cabinets
☐ I text/call while on the toilet
☐ I pick my nose in the restroom
☐ I talk to myself while on the toilet

Doodles & Brilliant Thoughts Inspired by The Throne

Welcome to our Restroom

Please Seat Yourself!

Name: _____

Visting From: _____

Date: _____ Time: _____

Reason for Visit: _____

During Your Visit Did you...

☐ Play with your smartphone?
☐ Mess with your hair?
☐ Inspect your teeth for food?
☐ Check out your butt in the mirror?
☐ Check your zipper/fly?
☐ Read through this entire guest book?

Your Favorite Name(s) for this Room?

☐ Powder Room   ☐ The office
☐ Crapper   ☐ Can
☐ John   ☐ Other....

Please Tick All That Apply

☐ I take restroom selfies
☐ I snoop in medicine cabinets
☐ I text/call while on the toilet
☐ I pick my nose in the restroom
☐ I talk to myself while on the toilet

Doodles & Brilliant Thoughts Inspired by The Throne

Welcome to our Restroom
Please Seat Yourself!

Name: _____
Visting From: _____
Date: _____ Time: _____
Reason for Visit: _____

During Your Visit Did you...
- [ ] Play with your smartphone?
- [ ] Mess with your hair?
- [ ] Inspect your teeth for food?
- [ ] Check out your butt in the mirror?
- [ ] Check your zipper/fly?
- [ ] Read through this entire guest book?

Your Favorite Name(s) for this Room?
- [ ] Powder Room
- [ ] Crapper
- [ ] John
- [ ] The office
- [ ] Can
- [ ] Other....

Please Tick All That Apply
- [ ] I take restroom selfies
- [ ] I snoop in medicine cabinets
- [ ] I text/call while on the toilet
- [ ] I pick my nose in the restroom
- [ ] I talk to myself while on the toilet

Doodles & Brilliant Thoughts Inspired by The Throne

Welcome to our Restroom

Please Seat Yourself!

Name: _____

Visting From: _____

Date: _____ Time: _____

Reason for Visit: _____

During Your Visit Did you...

☐ Play with your smartphone?
☐ Mess with your hair?
☐ Inspect your teeth for food?
☐ Check out your butt in the mirror?
☐ Check your zipper/fly?
☐ Read through this entire guest book?

Your Favorite Name(s) for this Room?

☐ Powder Room
☐ Crapper
☐ John
☐ The office
☐ Can
☐ Other....

Please Tick All That Apply

☐ I take restroom selfies
☐ I snoop in medicine cabinets
☐ I text/call while on the toilet
☐ I pick my nose in the restroom
☐ I talk to myself while on the toilet

Doodles & Brilliant Thoughts Inspired by The Throne

Welcome to our Restroom

Please Seat Yourself!

Name: _____
Visting From: _____
Date: _____ Time: _____
Reason for Visit: _____

During Your Visit Did you...

☐ Play with your smartphone?
☐ Mess with your hair?
☐ Inspect your teeth for food?
☐ Check out your butt in the mirror?
☐ Check your zipper/fly?
☐ Read through this entire guest book?

Your Favorite Name(s) for this Room?

☐ Powder Room   ☐ The office
☐ Crapper   ☐ Can
☐ John   ☐ Other....

Please Tick All That Apply

☐ I take restroom selfies
☐ I snoop in medicine cabinets
☐ I text/call while on the toilet
☐ I pick my nose in the restroom
☐ I talk to myself while on the toilet

Doodles & Brilliant Thoughts Inspired by The Throne

Welcome to our Restroom

Please Seat Yourself!

Name: _____

Visting From: _____

Date: _____ Time: _____

Reason for Visit: _____

During Your Visit Did you...

- ☐ Play with your smartphone?
- ☐ Mess with your hair?
- ☐ Inspect your teeth for food?
- ☐ Check out your butt in the mirror?
- ☐ Check your zipper/fly?
- ☐ Read through this entire guest book?

Your Favorite Name(s) for this Room?

- ☐ Powder Room
- ☐ Crapper
- ☐ John
- ☐ The office
- ☐ Can
- ☐ Other....

Please Tick All That Apply

- ☐ I take restroom selfies
- ☐ I snoop in medicine cabinets
- ☐ I text/call while on the toilet
- ☐ I pick my nose in the restroom
- ☐ I talk to myself while on the toilet

Doodles & Brilliant Thoughts Inspired by The Throne

Welcome to our Restroom
Please Seat Yourself!

Name: ――――――――――――――
Visiting From: ―――――――――――
Date: ――――――― Time: ―――――――
Reason for Visit: ―――――――――

During Your Visit Did you...

☐ Play with your smartphone?
☐ Mess with your hair?
☐ Inspect your teeth for food?
☐ Check out your butt in the mirror?
☐ Check your zipper/fly?
☐ Read through this entire guest book?

Your Favorite Name(s) for this Room?

☐ Powder Room
☐ Crapper
☐ John
☐ The office
☐ Can
☐ Other....

Please Tick All That Apply

☐ I take restroom selfies
☐ I snoop in medicine cabinets
☐ I text/call while on the toilet
☐ I pick my nose in the restroom
☐ I talk to myself while on the toilet

Doodles & Brilliant Thoughts Inspired by The Throne

Welcome to our Restroom
Please Seat Yourself!

Name: _____

Visting From: _____

Date: _____ Time: _____

Reason for Visit: _____

During Your Visit Did you...

☐ Play with your smartphone?
☐ Mess with your hair?
☐ Inspect your teeth for food?
☐ Check out your butt in the mirror?
☐ Check your zipper/fly?
☐ Read through this entire guest book?

Your Favorite Name(s) for this Room?

☐ Powder Room   ☐ The office
☐ Crapper   ☐ Can
☐ John   ☐ Other....

Please Tick All That Apply

☐ I take restroom selfies
☐ I snoop in medicine cabinets
☐ I text/call while on the toilet
☐ I pick my nose in the restroom
☐ I talk to myself while on the toilet

Doodles & Brilliant Thoughts Inspired by The Throne

Welcome to our Restroom

Please Seat Yourself!

Name: —————————————————
Visting From: ————————————
Date: ————————— Time: ——————
Reason for Visit: ——————————

During Your Visit Did you...

☐ Play with your smartphone?
☐ Mess with your hair?
☐ Inspect your teeth for food?
☐ Check out your butt in the mirror?
☐ Check your zipper/fly?
☐ Read through this entire guest book?

Your Favorite Name(s) for this Room?

☐ Powder Room ☐ The office
☐ Crapper   ☐ Can
☐ John   ☐ Other....

Please Tick All That Apply

☐ I take restroom selfies
☐ I snoop in medicine cabinets
☐ I text/call while on the toilet
☐ I pick my nose in the restroom
☐ I talk to myself while on the toilet

Doodles & Brilliant Thoughts Inspired by The Throne

Welcome to our Restroom

Please Seat Yourself!

Name: —————————————————————
Visting From: ————————————————
Date:————————— Time: ——————————
Reason for Visit: ——————————————

During Your Visit Did you...

☐ Play with your smartphone?
☐ Mess with your hair?
☐ Inspect your teeth for food?
☐ Check out your butt in the mirror?
☐ Check your zipper/fly?
☐ Read through this entire guest book?

Your Favorite Name(s) for this Room?

☐ Powder Room
☐ Crapper
☐ John
☐ The office
☐ Can
☐ Other....

Please Tick All That Apply

☐ I take restroom selfies
☐ I snoop in medicine cabinets
☐ I text/call while on the toilet
☐ I pick my nose in the restroom
☐ I talk to myself while on the toilet

Doodles & Brilliant Thoughts Inspired by The Throne

Welcome to our Restroom
Please Seat Yourself!

Name: _____

Visting From: _____

Date: _____ Time: _____

Reason for Visit: _____

During Your Visit Did you...

☐ Play with your smartphone?
☐ Mess with your hair?
☐ Inspect your teeth for food?
☐ Check out your butt in the mirror?
☐ Check your zipper/fly?
☐ Read through this entire guest book?

Your Favorite Name(s) for this Room?

☐ Powder Room   ☐ The office
☐ Crapper   ☐ Can
☐ John   ☐ Other....

Please Tick All That Apply

☐ I take restroom selfies
☐ I snoop in medicine cabinets
☐ I text/call while on the toilet
☐ I pick my nose in the restroom
☐ I talk to myself while on the toilet

Doodles & Brilliant Thoughts Inspired by The Throne

Welcome to our Restroom
Please Seat Yourself!

Name: ————————————————
Visting From: ————————————
Date: ——————— Time: —————
Reason for Visit: ————————————

During Your Visit Did you...

☐ Play with your smartphone?
☐ Mess with your hair?
☐ Inspect your teeth for food?
☐ Check out your butt in the mirror?
☐ Check your zipper/fly?
☐ Read through this entire guest book?

Your Favorite Name(s) for this Room?

☐ Powder Room   ☐ The office
☐ Crapper   ☐ Can
☐ John   ☐ Other....

Please Tick All That Apply

☐ I take restroom selfies
☐ I snoop in medicine cabinets
☐ I text/call while on the toilet
☐ I pick my nose in the restroom
☐ I talk to myself while on the toilet

Doodles & Brilliant Thoughts Inspired by The Throne

Welcome to our Restroom
Please Seat Yourself!

Name: _____
Visting From: _____
Date: _____ Time: _____
Reason for Visit: _____

During Your Visit Did you...

☐ Play with your smartphone?
☐ Mess with your hair?
☐ Inspect your teeth for food?
☐ Check out your butt in the mirror?
☐ Check your zipper/fly?
☐ Read through this entire guest book?

Your Favorite Name(s) for this Room?

☐ Powder Room ☐ The office
☐ Crapper   ☐ Can
☐ John   ☐ Other....

Please Tick All That Apply

☐ I take restroom selfies
☐ I snoop in medicine cabinets
☐ I text/call while on the toilet
☐ I pick my nose in the restroom
☐ I talk to myself while on the toilet

Doodles & Brilliant Thoughts Inspired by The Throne

Welcome to our Restroom
Please Seat Yourself!

Name: _____
Visting From: _____
Date: _____ Time: _____
Reason for Visit: _____

Your Favorite Name(s) for this Room?

- ☐ Powder Room
- ☐ Crapper
- ☐ John
- ☐ The office
- ☐ Can
- ☐ Other....

During Your Visit Did you...

- ☐ Play with your smartphone?
- ☐ Mess with your hair?
- ☐ Inspect your teeth for food?
- ☐ Check out your butt in the mirror?
- ☐ Check your zipper/fly?
- ☐ Read through this entire guest book?

Please Tick All That Apply

- ☐ I take restroom selfies
- ☐ I snoop in medicine cabinets
- ☐ I text/call while on the toilet
- ☐ I pick my nose in the restroom
- ☐ I talk to myself while on the toilet

Doodles & Brilliant Thoughts Inspired by The Throne

Welcome to our Restroom

Please Seat Yourself!

Name: —————————————————
Visting From: —————————————
Date:————————— Time: ————————
Reason for Visit: ——————————————

During Your Visit Did you...

- ☐ Play with your smartphone?
- ☐ Mess with your hair?
- ☐ Inspect your teeth for food?
- ☐ Check out your butt in the mirror?
- ☐ Check your zipper/fly?
- ☐ Read through this entire guest book?

Your Favorite Name(s) for this Room?

- ☐ Powder Room
- ☐ Crapper
- ☐ John
- ☐ The office
- ☐ Can
- ☐ Other....

Please Tick All That Apply

- ☐ I take restroom selfies
- ☐ I snoop in medicine cabinets
- ☐ I text/call while on the toilet
- ☐ I pick my nose in the restroom
- ☐ I talk to myself while on the toilet

Doodles & Brilliant Thoughts Inspired by The Throne

Welcome to our Restroom
Please Seat Yourself!

Name: _____
Visting From: _____
Date: _____ Time: _____
Reason for Visit: _____

During Your Visit Did you...

- ☐ Play with your smartphone?
- ☐ Mess with your hair?
- ☐ Inspect your teeth for food?
- ☐ Check out your butt in the mirror?
- ☐ Check your zipper/fly?
- ☐ Read through this entire guest book?

Your Favorite Name(s) for this Room?

- ☐ Powder Room
- ☐ Crapper
- ☐ John
- ☐ The office
- ☐ Can
- ☐ Other....

Please Tick All That Apply

- ☐ I take restroom selfies
- ☐ I snoop in medicine cabinets
- ☐ I text/call while on the toilet
- ☐ I pick my nose in the restroom
- ☐ I talk to myself while on the toilet

Doodles & Brilliant Thoughts Inspired by The Throne

Welcome to our Restroom

Please Seat Yourself!

Name: _____
Visiting From: _____
Date: _____ Time: _____
Reason for Visit: _____

During Your Visit Did you...

- ☐ Play with your smartphone?
- ☐ Mess with your hair?
- ☐ Inspect your teeth for food?
- ☐ Check out your butt in the mirror?
- ☐ Check your zipper/fly?
- ☐ Read through this entire guest book?

Your Favorite Name(s) for this Room?

- ☐ Powder Room
- ☐ Crapper
- ☐ John
- ☐ The office
- ☐ Can
- ☐ Other....

Please Tick All That Apply

- ☐ I take restroom selfies
- ☐ I snoop in medicine cabinets
- ☐ I text/call while on the toilet
- ☐ I pick my nose in the restroom
- ☐ I talk to myself while on the toilet

Doodles & Brilliant Thoughts Inspired by The Throne

Welcome to our Restroom

Please Seat Yourself!

Name: ─────────────────
Visting From: ─────────────
Date:───────── Time: ──────────
Reason for Visit: ──────────────

During Your Visit Did you...

☐ Play with your smartphone?
☐ Mess with your hair?
☐ Inspect your teeth for food?
☐ Check out your butt in the mirror?
☐ Check your zipper/fly?
☐ Read through this entire guest book?

Your Favorite Name(s) for this Room?

☐ Powder Room   ☐ The office
☐ Crapper   ☐ Can
☐ John   ☐ Other....

Please Tick All That Apply

☐ I take restroom selfies
☐ I snoop in medicine cabinets
☐ I text/call while on the toilet
☐ I pick my nose in the restroom
☐ I talk to myself while on the toilet

Doodles & Brilliant Thoughts Inspired by The Throne

Welcome to our Restroom
Please Seat Yourself!

Name: ——————————————
Visiting From: ——————————————
Date: ——————— Time: —————————
Reason for Visit: ————————————

During Your Visit Did you...

- ☐ Play with your smartphone?
- ☐ Mess with your hair?
- ☐ Inspect your teeth for food?
- ☐ Check out your butt in the mirror?
- ☐ Check your zipper/fly?
- ☐ Read through this entire guest book?

Your Favorite Name(s) for this Room?

- ☐ Powder Room
- ☐ Crapper
- ☐ John
- ☐ The office
- ☐ Can
- ☐ Other....

Please Tick All That Apply

- ☐ I take restroom selfies
- ☐ I snoop in medicine cabinets
- ☐ I text/call while on the toilet
- ☐ I pick my nose in the restroom
- ☐ I talk to myself while on the toilet

Doodles & Brilliant Thoughts Inspired by The Throne

Welcome to our Restroom
Please Seat Yourself!

Name: —————————————————
Visiting From: ————————————
Date: ——————— Time: —————
Reason for Visit: ————————————

During Your Visit Did you...

- [ ] Play with your smartphone?
- [ ] Mess with your hair?
- [ ] Inspect your teeth for food?
- [ ] Check out your butt in the mirror?
- [ ] Check your zipper/fly?
- [ ] Read through this entire guest book?

Your Favorite Name(s) for this Room?

- [ ] Powder Room
- [ ] Crapper
- [ ] John
- [ ] The office
- [ ] Can
- [ ] Other....

Please Tick All That Apply

- [ ] I take restroom selfies
- [ ] I snoop in medicine cabinets
- [ ] I text/call while on the toilet
- [ ] I pick my nose in the restroom
- [ ] I talk to myself while on the toilet

Doodles & Brilliant Thoughts Inspired by The Throne

Welcome to our Restroom
Please Seat Yourself!

Name: _____
Visting From: _____
Date: _____ Time: _____
Reason for Visit: _____

During Your Visit Did you...

☐ Play with your smartphone?
☐ Mess with your hair?
☐ Inspect your teeth for food?
☐ Check out your butt in the mirror?
☐ Check your zipper/fly?
☐ Read through this entire guest book?

Your Favorite Name(s) for this Room?

☐ Powder Room   ☐ The office
☐ Crapper   ☐ Can
☐ John   ☐ Other....

Please Tick All That Apply

☐ I take restroom selfies
☐ I snoop in medicine cabinets
☐ I text/call while on the toilet
☐ I pick my nose in the restroom
☐ I talk to myself while on the toilet

Doodles & Brilliant Thoughts Inspired by The Throne

Welcome to our Restroom

Please Seat Yourself!

Name: _____
Visting From: _____
Date: _____ Time: _____
Reason for Visit: _____

During Your Visit Did you...

☐ Play with your smartphone?
☐ Mess with your hair?
☐ Inspect your teeth for food?
☐ Check out your butt in the mirror?
☐ Check your zipper/fly?
☐ Read through this entire guest book?

Your Favorite Name(s) for this Room?

☐ Powder Room
☐ Crapper
☐ John
☐ The office
☐ Can
☐ Other....

Please Tick All That Apply

☐ I take restroom selfies
☐ I snoop in medicine cabinets
☐ I text/call while on the toilet
☐ I pick my nose in the restroom
☐ I talk to myself while on the toilet

Doodles & Brilliant Thoughts Inspired by The Throne

Welcome to our Restroom

Please Seat Yourself!

Name: —————————————————
Visiting From: —————————————————
Date: ————————— Time: ——————————
Reason for Visit: —————————————

During Your Visit Did you...

☐ Play with your smartphone?
☐ Mess with your hair?
☐ Inspect your teeth for food?
☐ Check out your butt in the mirror?
☐ Check your zipper/fly?
☐ Read through this entire guest book?

Your Favorite Name(s) for this Room?

☐ Powder Room   ☐ The office
☐ Crapper   ☐ Can
☐ John   ☐ Other....

Please Tick All That Apply

☐ I take restroom selfies
☐ I snoop in medicine cabinets
☐ I text/call while on the toilet
☐ I pick my nose in the restroom
☐ I talk to myself while on the toilet

Doodles & Brilliant Thoughts Inspired by The Throne

Welcome to our Restroom

Please Seat Yourself!

Name: ―――――――――――――
Visiting From: ―――――――――
Date: ――――――― Time: ―――――
Reason for Visit: ―――――――――

During Your Visit Did you...

☐ Play with your smartphone?
☐ Mess with your hair?
☐ Inspect your teeth for food?
☐ Check out your butt in the mirror?
☐ Check your zipper/fly?
☐ Read through this entire guest book?

Your Favorite Name(s) for this Room?

☐ Powder Room
☐ Crapper
☐ John
☐ The office
☐ Can
☐ Other....

Please Tick All That Apply

☐ I take restroom selfies
☐ I snoop in medicine cabinets
☐ I text/call while on the toilet
☐ I pick my nose in the restroom
☐ I talk to myself while on the toilet

Doodles & Brilliant Thoughts Inspired by The Throne

Welcome to our Restroom

Please Seat Yourself!

Name: _____

Visting From: _____

Date: _____ Time: _____

Reason for Visit: _____

During Your Visit Did you...

☐ Play with your smartphone?
☐ Mess with your hair?
☐ Inspect your teeth for food?
☐ Check out your butt in the mirror?
☐ Check your zipper/fly?
☐ Read through this entire guest book?

Your Favorite Name(s) for this Room?

☐ Powder Room
☐ Crapper
☐ John
☐ The office
☐ Can
☐ Other....

Please Tick All That Apply

☐ I take restroom selfies
☐ I snoop in medicine cabinets
☐ I text/call while on the toilet
☐ I pick my nose in the restroom
☐ I talk to myself while on the toilet

Doodles & Brilliant Thoughts Inspired by The Throne

Welcome to our Restroom

Please Seat Yourself!

Name: _____
Visting From: _____
Date: _____ Time: _____
Reason for Visit: _____

Your Favorite Name(s) for this Room?

- ☐ Powder Room
- ☐ Crapper
- ☐ John
- ☐ The office
- ☐ Can
- ☐ Other....

During Your Visit Did you...

- ☐ Play with your smartphone?
- ☐ Mess with your hair?
- ☐ Inspect your teeth for food?
- ☐ Check out your butt in the mirror?
- ☐ Check your zipper/fly?
- ☐ Read through this entire guest book?

Please Tick All That Apply

- ☐ I take restroom selfies
- ☐ I snoop in medicine cabinets
- ☐ I text/call while on the toilet
- ☐ I pick my nose in the restroom
- ☐ I talk to myself while on the toilet

Doodles & Brilliant Thoughts Inspired by The Throne

Welcome to our Restroom
Please Seat Yourself!

Name: _____
Visting From: _____
Date: _____ Time: _____
Reason for Visit: _____

During Your Visit Did you...

- ☐ Play with your smartphone?
- ☐ Mess with your hair?
- ☐ Inspect your teeth for food?
- ☐ Check out your butt in the mirror?
- ☐ Check your zipper/fly?
- ☐ Read through this entire guest book?

Your Favorite Name(s) for this Room?

- ☐ Powder Room
- ☐ Crapper
- ☐ John
- ☐ The office
- ☐ Can
- ☐ Other....

Please Tick All That Apply

- ☐ I take restroom selfies
- ☐ I snoop in medicine cabinets
- ☐ I text/call while on the toilet
- ☐ I pick my nose in the restroom
- ☐ I talk to myself while on the toilet

Doodles & Brilliant Thoughts Inspired by The Throne

Welcome to our Restroom
Please Seat Yourself!

Name: _____
Visting From: _____
Date: _____ Time: _____
Reason for Visit: _____

During Your Visit Did you...

☐ Play with your smartphone?
☐ Mess with your hair?
☐ Inspect your teeth for food?
☐ Check out your butt in the mirror?
☐ Check your zipper/fly?
☐ Read through this entire guest book?

Your Favorite Name(s) for this Room?

☐ Powder Room ☐ The office
☐ Crapper ☐ Can
☐ John ☐ Other....

Please Tick All That Apply

☐ I take restroom selfies
☐ I snoop in medicine cabinets
☐ I text/call while on the toilet
☐ I pick my nose in the restroom
☐ I talk to myself while on the toilet

Doodles & Brilliant Thoughts Inspired by The Throne

Welcome to our Restroom
Please Seat Yourself!

Name: _____
Visiting From: _____
Date: _____ Time: _____
Reason for Visit: _____

During Your Visit Did you...

- ☐ Play with your smartphone?
- ☐ Mess with your hair?
- ☐ Inspect your teeth for food?
- ☐ Check out your butt in the mirror?
- ☐ Check your zipper/fly?
- ☐ Read through this entire guest book?

Your Favorite Name(s) for this Room?

- ☐ Powder Room
- ☐ Crapper
- ☐ John
- ☐ The office
- ☐ Can
- ☐ Other....

Please Tick All That Apply

- ☐ I take restroom selfies
- ☐ I snoop in medicine cabinets
- ☐ I text/call while on the toilet
- ☐ I pick my nose in the restroom
- ☐ I talk to myself while on the toilet

Doodles & Brilliant Thoughts Inspired by The Throne

Welcome to our Restroom
Please Seat Yourself!

Name: ───────────────
Visting From: ───────────
Date: ───────── Time: ──────────
Reason for Visit: ────────────

During Your Visit Did you...

- ☐ Play with your smartphone?
- ☐ Mess with your hair?
- ☐ Inspect your teeth for food?
- ☐ Check out your butt in the mirror?
- ☐ Check your zipper/fly?
- ☐ Read through this entire guest book?

Your Favorite Name(s) for this Room?

- ☐ Powder Room
- ☐ Crapper
- ☐ John
- ☐ The office
- ☐ Can
- ☐ Other....

Please Tick All That Apply

- ☐ I take restroom selfies
- ☐ I snoop in medicine cabinets
- ☐ I text/call while on the toilet
- ☐ I pick my nose in the restroom
- ☐ I talk to myself while on the toilet

Doodles & Brilliant Thoughts Inspired by The Throne

Welcome to our Restroom

Please Seat Yourself!

Name: ——————————————
Visiting From: ——————————
Date: ——————— Time: —————
Reason for Visit: ————————

During Your Visit Did you...

- [ ] Play with your smartphone?
- [ ] Mess with your hair?
- [ ] Inspect your teeth for food?
- [ ] Check out your butt in the mirror?
- [ ] Check your zipper/fly?
- [ ] Read through this entire guest book?

Your Favorite Name(s) for this Room?

- [ ] Powder Room
- [ ] Crapper
- [ ] John
- [ ] The office
- [ ] Can
- [ ] Other....

Please Tick All That Apply

- [ ] I take restroom selfies
- [ ] I snoop in medicine cabinets
- [ ] I text/call while on the toilet
- [ ] I pick my nose in the restroom
- [ ] I talk to myself while on the toilet

Doodles & Brilliant Thoughts Inspired by The Throne

Welcome to our Restroom
Please Seat Yourself!

Name: _____

Visting From: _____

Date: _____ Time: _____

Reason for Visit: _____

During Your Visit Did you...

☐ Play with your smartphone?
☐ Mess with your hair?
☐ Inspect your teeth for food?
☐ Check out your butt in the mirror?
☐ Check your zipper/fly?
☐ Read through this entire guest book?

Your Favorite Name(s) for this Room?

☐ Powder Room
☐ Crapper
☐ John
☐ The office
☐ Can
☐ Other....

Please Tick All That Apply

☐ I take restroom selfies
☐ I snoop in medicine cabinets
☐ I text/call while on the toilet
☐ I pick my nose in the restroom
☐ I talk to myself while on the toilet

Doodles & Brilliant Thoughts Inspired by The Throne

Welcome to our Restroom
Please Seat Yourself!

Name: ――――――――――――――
Visiting From: ――――――――――――
Date: ――――――――― Time: ―――――――
Reason for Visit: ――――――――――――

During Your Visit Did you...

☐ Play with your smartphone?
☐ Mess with your hair?
☐ Inspect your teeth for food?
☐ Check out your butt in the mirror?
☐ Check your zipper/fly?
☐ Read through this entire guest book?

Your Favorite Name(s) for this Room?

☐ Powder Room ☐ The office
☐ Crapper ☐ Can
☐ John ☐ Other....

Please Tick All That Apply

☐ I take restroom selfies
☐ I snoop in medicine cabinets
☐ I text/call while on the toilet
☐ I pick my nose in the restroom
☐ I talk to myself while on the toilet

Doodles & Brilliant Thoughts Inspired by The Throne

Welcome to our Restroom
Please Seat Yourself!

Name: _____

Visting From: _____

Date: _____ Time: _____

Reason for Visit: _____

During Your Visit Did you...

- ☐ Play with your smartphone?
- ☐ Mess with your hair?
- ☐ Inspect your teeth for food?
- ☐ Check out your butt in the mirror?
- ☐ Check your zipper/fly?
- ☐ Read through this entire guest book?

Your Favorite Name(s) for this Room?

- ☐ Powder Room
- ☐ Crapper
- ☐ John
- ☐ The office
- ☐ Can
- ☐ Other....

Please Tick All That Apply

- ☐ I take restroom selfies
- ☐ I snoop in medicine cabinets
- ☐ I text/call while on the toilet
- ☐ I pick my nose in the restroom
- ☐ I talk to myself while on the toilet

Doodles & Brilliant Thoughts Inspired by The Throne

Welcome to our Restroom
Please Seat Yourself!

Name: _____
Visting From: _____
Date: _____ Time: _____
Reason for Visit: _____

During Your Visit Did you...

- ☐ Play with your smartphone?
- ☐ Mess with your hair?
- ☐ Inspect your teeth for food?
- ☐ Check out your butt in the mirror?
- ☐ Check your zipper/fly?
- ☐ Read through this entire guest book?

Your Favorite Name(s) for this Room?

- ☐ Powder Room
- ☐ Crapper
- ☐ John
- ☐ The office
- ☐ Can
- ☐ Other....

Please Tick All That Apply

- ☐ I take restroom selfies
- ☐ I snoop in medicine cabinets
- ☐ I text/call while on the toilet
- ☐ I pick my nose in the restroom
- ☐ I talk to myself while on the toilet

Doodles & Brilliant Thoughts Inspired by The Throne

Welcome to our Restroom
Please Seat Yourself!

Name: —————————————————
Visiting From: —————————————
Date: —————————— Time: ——————
Reason for Visit: ———————————

During Your Visit Did you...

- [ ] Play with your smartphone?
- [ ] Mess with your hair?
- [ ] Inspect your teeth for food?
- [ ] Check out your butt in the mirror?
- [ ] Check your zipper/fly?
- [ ] Read through this entire guest book?

Your Favorite Name(s) for this Room?

- [ ] Powder Room
- [ ] Crapper
- [ ] John
- [ ] The office
- [ ] Can
- [ ] Other....

Please Tick All That Apply

- [ ] I take restroom selfies
- [ ] I snoop in medicine cabinets
- [ ] I text/call while on the toilet
- [ ] I pick my nose in the restroom
- [ ] I talk to myself while on the toilet

Doodles & Brilliant Thoughts Inspired by The Throne

Welcome to our Restroom
Please Seat Yourself!

Name: _____
Visting From: _____
Date: _____ Time: _____
Reason for Visit: _____

During Your Visit Did you...

☐ Play with your smartphone?
☐ Mess with your hair?
☐ Inspect your teeth for food?
☐ Check out your butt in the mirror?
☐ Check your zipper/fly?
☐ Read through this entire guest book?

Your Favorite Name(s) for this Room?

☐ Powder Room
☐ Crapper
☐ John
☐ The office
☐ Can
☐ Other....

Please Tick All That Apply

☐ I take restroom selfies
☐ I snoop in medicine cabinets
☐ I text/call while on the toilet
☐ I pick my nose in the restroom
☐ I talk to myself while on the toilet

Doodles & Brilliant Thoughts Inspired by The Throne

Welcome to our Restroom
Please Seat Yourself!

Name: _____
Visting From: _____
Date: _____ Time: _____
Reason for Visit: _____

During Your Visit Did you...

☐ Play with your smartphone?
☐ Mess with your hair?
☐ Inspect your teeth for food?
☐ Check out your butt in the mirror?
☐ Check your zipper/fly?
☐ Read through this entire guest book?

Your Favorite Name(s) for this Room?

☐ Powder Room   ☐ The office
☐ Crapper   ☐ Can
☐ John   ☐ Other....

Please Tick All That Apply

☐ I take restroom selfies
☐ I snoop in medicine cabinets
☐ I text/call while on the toilet
☐ I pick my nose in the restroom
☐ I talk to myself while on the toilet

Doodles & Brilliant Thoughts Inspired by The Throne

Welcome to our Restroom
Please Seat Yourself!

Name: —————————————
Visiting From: ————————————
Date: ——————— Time: ——————
Reason for Visit: ——————————

During Your Visit Did you...

- ☐ Play with your smartphone?
- ☐ Mess with your hair?
- ☐ Inspect your teeth for food?
- ☐ Check out your butt in the mirror?
- ☐ Check your zipper/fly?
- ☐ Read through this entire guest book?

Your Favorite Name(s) for this Room?

- ☐ Powder Room
- ☐ Crapper
- ☐ John
- ☐ The office
- ☐ Can
- ☐ Other....

Please Tick All That Apply

- ☐ I take restroom selfies
- ☐ I snoop in medicine cabinets
- ☐ I text/call while on the toilet
- ☐ I pick my nose in the restroom
- ☐ I talk to myself while on the toilet

Doodles & Brilliant Thoughts Inspired by The Throne

Welcome to our Restroom
Please Seat Yourself!

Name: _____
Visiting From: _____
Date: _____ Time: _____
Reason for Visit: _____

Your Favorite Name(s) for this Room?

☐ Powder Room   ☐ The office
☐ Crapper   ☐ Can
☐ John   ☐ Other....

During Your Visit Did you...

☐ Play with your smartphone?
☐ Mess with your hair?
☐ Inspect your teeth for food?
☐ Check out your butt in the mirror?
☐ Check your zipper/fly?
☐ Read through this entire guest book?

Please Tick All That Apply

☐ I take restroom selfies
☐ I snoop in medicine cabinets
☐ I text/call while on the toilet
☐ I pick my nose in the restroom
☐ I talk to myself while on the toilet

Doodles & Brilliant Thoughts Inspired by The Throne

Welcome to our Restroom
Please Seat Yourself!

Name: ————————————————
Visting From: ————————————————
Date:———————————— Time: ————————
Reason for Visit: ————————————————

During Your Visit Did you...

- ☐ Play with your smartphone?
- ☐ Mess with your hair?
- ☐ Inspect your teeth for food?
- ☐ Check out your butt in the mirror?
- ☐ Check your zipper/fly?
- ☐ Read through this entire guest book?

Your Favorite Name(s) for this Room?

- ☐ Powder Room
- ☐ Crapper
- ☐ John
- ☐ The office
- ☐ Can
- ☐ Other....

Please Tick All That Apply

- ☐ I take restroom selfies
- ☐ I snoop in medicine cabinets
- ☐ I text/call while on the toilet
- ☐ I pick my nose in the restroom
- ☐ I talk to myself while on the toilet

Doodles & Brilliant Thoughts Inspired by The Throne

Welcome to our Restroom

Please Seat Yourself!

Name: _____
Visting From: _____
Date: _____ Time: _____
Reason for Visit: _____

During Your Visit Did you...

☐ Play with your smartphone?
☐ Mess with your hair?
☐ Inspect your teeth for food?
☐ Check out your butt in the mirror?
☐ Check your zipper/fly?
☐ Read through this entire guest book?

Your Favorite Name(s) for this Room?

☐ Powder Room   ☐ The office
☐ Crapper   ☐ Can
☐ John   ☐ Other....

Please Tick All That Apply

☐ I take restroom selfies
☐ I snoop in medicine cabinets
☐ I text/call while on the toilet
☐ I pick my nose in the restroom
☐ I talk to myself while on the toilet

Doodles & Brilliant Thoughts Inspired by The Throne

Welcome to our Restroom
Please Seat Yourself!

Name: ————————————
Visiting From: ————————————
Date: ———————— **Time:** ——————
Reason for Visit: ————————————

During Your Visit Did you...

☐ Play with your smartphone?
☐ Mess with your hair?
☐ Inspect your teeth for food?
☐ Check out your butt in the mirror?
☐ Check your zipper/fly?
☐ Read through this entire guest book?

Your Favorite Name(s) for this Room?

☐ Powder Room   ☐ The office
☐ Crapper   ☐ Can
☐ John   ☐ Other....

Please Tick All That Apply

☐ I take restroom selfies
☐ I snoop in medicine cabinets
☐ I text/call while on the toilet
☐ I pick my nose in the restroom
☐ I talk to myself while on the toilet

Doodles & Brilliant Thoughts Inspired by The Throne

Made in the USA
San Bernardino, CA
29 November 2019

60590347R00058